CHRISTMAS
in the
COUNTRY

By Barbara Collyer and John R. Foley

Illustrated by Retta Worcester

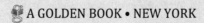 A GOLDEN BOOK · NEW YORK

Christmas was coming!

And as if that were not exciting enough, Betty, Bob, and their parents were going to the country to spend Christmas with Grandmother and Grandfather.

When they arrived at the train station, there were hugs and kisses all around, and then they all piled into Grandfather's sleigh.

The sleigh bells went tinkle-tinkle, the horses went snort-snort, and off they rode down the snowy village streets till Grandfather said, "Whoa."

Soon they were greeting Grandmother at the door of the cozy farmhouse.

"My, how you've grown!" she said. "Come along now and get washed up."

"I have some important business with Bob over
at the edge of the pasture," Grandfather said.
"What is it? May I come, too?" Betty asked.

"It's a secret," Grandfather said very mysteriously.
"Never you mind, child," Grandmother said. "You
come along to the kitchen. I have a secret for you, too."

Chop! Chop! Chop! went the secret in the pasture.

Stitch! Stitch! Stitch! went the secret in the kitchen.

What a wonderful busy time there was after
dinner, with the lights to put on the Christmas tree,
and the boxes of colored balls and angels and stars!

And Betty hung her cranberry chain on the tree
by herself!

Then the family gathered around the old organ
to sing carols.

But it had been a long, busy day, and Betty's eyes began to close. And before the last notes of "Silent Night" were sung, she was fast asleep in Grandmother's rocker!

So Grandfather carried Betty up to bed.
And Grandmother took Bob by the hand.

"Grandmother," Bob asked, when he was ready to be tucked in bed, "who else is getting ready for Christmas the way we are?"

"Why," said Grandmother, "I daresay, over in the barn at this very moment, the animals are getting ready for Christmas.

"Perhaps they're having a tree of their own, and, of course, the hens would be making corn garlands for it, just as Betty made her cranberry chain.

"And who'd do better at trimming the tree than
the pigeons who live in the loft?

"And the pigs, well, they'd surely be seeing to the goodies for the next day's feast . . . if they didn't eat them all up themselves.

"And the cows might be wrapping up presents.
My, how handy their horns would be!

"The little lambs would give the wool for Christmas stockings. Perhaps they'd even learn to knit, since Christmas is a magical time.

"Even the littlest animals do their bit to help,
until at last it's time to go to sleep.

"And now it's time for this little one to go to sleep, too. For remember, everywhere—on Christmas Eve—

"to all good children

"Santa Claus comes!"